The BIG Green Book of Beginner Books

The BIG Green Book of Beginner Books

By **Dr. Seuss**

Illustrated by Quentin Blake, George Booth,
Roy McKie, Michael J. Smollin,
James Stevenson, and B. Tobey

RANDOM HOUSE 🏠 NEW YORK

Dr. Seuss's real name was Theodor Geisel. On books he wrote to be illustrated by others, he often used the name Theo. LeSieg, which is Geisel spelled backward.

Visit us on the Web!
Seussville.com
randomhousekids.com

Educators and librarians, for a variety of teaching tools, visit us at
RHTeachersLibrarians.com

ISBN: 978-0-375-85807-9

Library of Congress Control Number: 2009921975

Printed in the United States of America   36   35   34   33   32   31

Random House Children's Books supports the First Amendment and celebrates the right to read.

Contents

Great Day for Up   9

Would You Rather Be a Bullfrog?   39

I Wish That I Had Duck Feet   69

Wacky Wednesday   135

Maybe You Should Fly a Jet!
Maybe You Should Be a Vet!   175

I Am NOT Going to Get Up Today!   217

The BIG Green Book of Beginner Books

GREAT DAY for UP

By

Dr. Seuss

Pictures by
Quentin Blake

UP!
UP!

The sun is getting up.

The sun gets up.

So UP with you!

UP!

Ear number one . . .

Ear number two.

Up, heads!

Up, whiskers!

Tails!

Great day, today!
Great day
for

UP!

Up! Up!

You!
Open up
your eyes!

You worms!

You frogs!

You butterflies!

Up, whales!

Up, snails!

Up, rooster!

Hen!

18

Up!

Girls and women!

Boys and men!

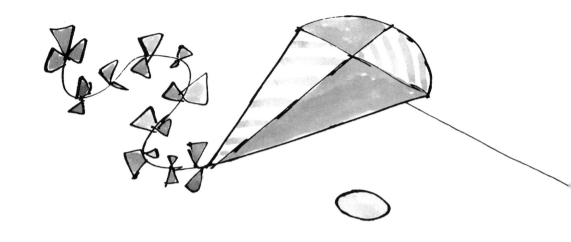

Great day
for UP FEET!
Lefts and rights.

And **Up! Up!** Baseballs!

Footballs! Kites!

Great day
to sing
up on a wire.

UP!

Up, voices!
Louder! Higher!

23

Up stairs!

Up ladders!

Up on stilts!

Great
day
for up
Mt. Dill-ma-dilts.

Everybody's doing UPs!

On bikes . . .

. . . and trees

. . . and buttercups.

Up! Up!

Waiters!

Alligators!

Up, folks!

Up in
elevators!

UP!

Up giraffes!

Great day
for seals!

Great day for UP
on ferris wheels!

UP! UP! UP!

Fill up the air.

Up, flags!
Balloons!
UP! Everywhere!

UP! UP! UP!

Great day for UP!

Wake every person,
pig and pup,
till EVERYONE
on Earth is up!

Except for me.
Please go away.
No up.
I'm sleeping in today.

Would you rather be a Bullfrog?

By **Dr. Seuss***

*writing as
Theo. LeSieg

Illustrated by *Roy McKie*

Tell me!

Would you rather be
a Dog . . . or be a Cat?

It's time for you
to think about
important things like that.

Would you
rather be
a Bullfrog . . .

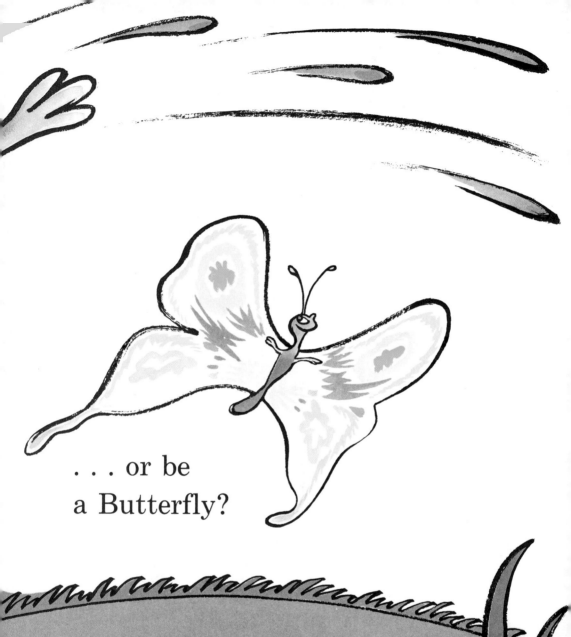

. . . or be
a Butterfly?

Which one
would you rather be?
Come on, now.
Tell me why.

Tell me.
Would you rather be
a Minnow
or a Whale?

And tell me,
would you
rather be
a Hammer
or a Nail?

Would you
rather have
a Feather . . .

or a Bushy Tail behind?

Which would feel
the best on you?
Come on!
Make up your mind.

And . . .
would you rather be
a Cactus . . .

or a Toadstool . . .

or a Rose?

AND . . .
which would look
the best on you . . .

. . . the Long
or
Shortish Nose?

Would you
rather
be
a Skinny . . .

OR
would you rather be
a FAT?

Would you rather
be a Ball . . .

. . . or
would you
rather be
a Bat?

And once more
I'm going to ask you . . .
how about
that Dog and Cat?

THINK, now!
Would you rather be

. . . a Rooster

. . . or a Hen?

(How would you like to
lay an egg
every now and then?)

Would you
rather have
big Moose Horns . . .

. . . or small horns
like a Cow?

This is so, so, so important
and I want
to know right now!

Would you
rather be
a Bloogle Bird
and fly around
and sing . . .

. . . or would you
rather be
a Bumble Bee
and fly around
and sting?

And tell me,
would you rather be
a Table . . . or a Chair?

And NOW tell me,
would you rather have
Green . . . or Purple Hair?

53

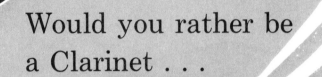

Would you rather be
a Clarinet . . .

. . . a Trombone

. . . or a Drum?

(How would you
like to have someone
going BOOM-BOOM
on your Tum?)

Suppose you had to be
a LETTER!
Well, then,
which one would you be?
Would you rather be a Curly one . . .

. . . like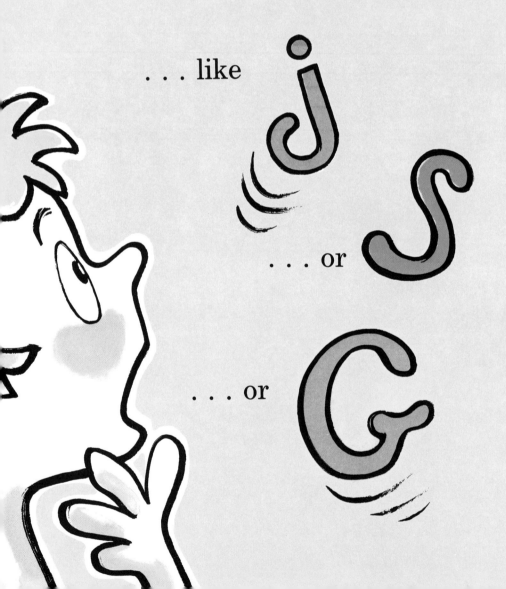

. . . or

. . . or

Or would you rather
be a Sharpie . . .

. . . like **K**

. . . or **Z**

. . . or **V**

Now tell me . . .
would you rather be
a Window . . . or . . . a Door?

And would you
have more fun

if you had Six Feet . . .

or a Hundred and Sixty-four?

These are
real important questions.
Come on!
Tell me! Tell me please!

Would you
rather be
a Soda?

OR . . . .

A piece
of smelly
Cheese?

Would you rather
live in Igloos . . . or . . .
would you
rather live in Tents?

AND . . .

Would you
rather be
a Dollar Bill

. . . or Ninety-seven Cents?

AND would you rather be
a Mermaid
with a tail instead of feet . . . ?

OR . . .

Would you rather be
a Spook
and run around
dressed in a sheet?

Would you
rather be
a Jellyfish . . .

. . . a Sawfish . . .

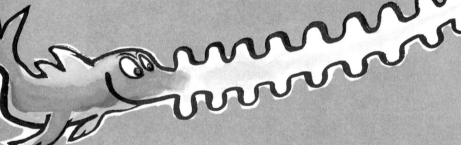

. . . or Sardine?

AND
would
you
rather be
THIS Thing . . . or THAT . . .

or
the
Thing
that's
in between?

It's hard to make your mind up
about important things like that.

(I can't even make
MY mind up
about that
Dog and Cat.)

I WISH
that I had
DUCK FEET

By **Dr. Seuss***

*writing as
Theo. LeSieg

Illustrated by **BTOBEY-**

I wish

that I had duck feet.

And I can tell you why.

You can splash around in duck feet.

You don't have to keep them dry.

I wish that I had duck feet.
No more shoes!
No shoes for me!
The man down at the shoe store
would not have my size, you see.

If I had two duck feet,
I could laugh at Big Bill Brown.
I would say, "YOU don't have duck feet!
These are all there are in town!"

I think it would be very good
to have them when I play.
Only kids with duck feet on
can ever play this way.

BUT . . .

My mother would not like them.

She would say, "Get off my floor!"

She would say, "You take your duck feet

and you take them out that door!

"Don't ever come in here again
with duck feet on. Now, DON'T."
SO . . .
I guess I can't have duck feet.
I would like to. But I won't.

SO . . .

If I can't have duck feet,

I'll have something else instead . . .

Say!

I know what!

I wish I had

two horns up on my head!

I wish I had two deer horns.
They would be a lot of fun.
Then I could wear
ten hats up there!
Big Bill can just wear one.

I think they would
be very good
to have when I play ball.
Then nobody could stop me.
No, sir! Nobody at all!

My horns could carry
books and stuff
like paper, pens and strings
and apples for my teacher
and a lot of other things!

BUT . . .
If I had
big deer horns,
I would never
get a ride.

I could never ride the school bus.
I could never get inside!

AND SO . . .

I won't have deer horns.

I'll have something else instead.

I wish I had a whale spout.

A whale spout on my head!

When days get hot
it would be good
to spout my spout in school.

And then Miss Banks
would say, "Thanks! Thanks!
You keep our school so cool."

I could play all day in summer.
I would never feel the heat.

I would beat Big Bill at tennis.
I would play him off his feet.

BUT . . .

My mother would not like it.

I know just what she would say:

"Not in the house!

You shut that off!

You take that spout away."

I know that she would tell me,
"I don't want that spout about!"
And when Mother
does not want a thing,
it's O—U—T. It's out!

AND SO . . .

I will not have one.

I don't wish to be a whale.

I think
it would be better
if I had
a long, long tail.

I wish I had a long, long tail.

Some day I will. I hope.

And then I'll show

the kids in town

new ways to jump a rope!

If I had a long, long tail
I know what I would like.
I would like to ride down State Street
pulling girls behind my bike.

I wish I had a long, long tail.
And I can tell you why.
I could hit a fly ten feet away
and hit him in the eye.

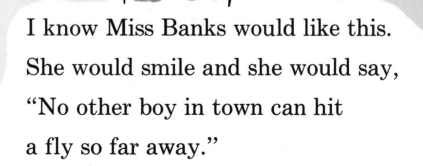

I know Miss Banks would like this.

She would smile and she would say,

"No other boy in town can hit

a fly so far away."

BUT . . .
If I had a long, long tail,
I know that Big Bill Brown
would tie me in a tree!
He would!
Then how would I get down?

I don't think that I would like it
with my tail tied in a tree.
The more I think about it . . . NO!
No long, long tail for me.

AND SO . . .

If I can't have a tail,

I'll have a long, long nose!

A nose just like an elephant's,

the longest nose that grows.

I wish I had a long, long nose

and I can tell you why.

I think it would

be very good

to get at things up high.

Every kid in town would love it.
Every kid but Big Bill Brown.
And every time I saw him
I would sneeze
and blow him down.

KERCHOO!

Say!
I could help the firemen!
My nose would be just right.
I could help them put out fires
a hundred times a night.

Oh, I would do a lot of things
that no one ever did.
And everyone in town would say,
"Just watch that long-nose kid!"

BUT . . .

If I had a long, long nose,

I know what Dad would do.

My dad would make me wash the car!

The house and windows, too!

117

My dad would make me work all day
and wash things with that hose!
I guess it would not be so good
to have a long, long nose.

NOW . . .

Let me think about it.

All these things I want are bad.

And so I wish . . .

I wish . . . I wish . . .

What DO I wish I had? . . .

I know what!
I know just what!
I know just what to do!
I WISH THAT I HAD ALL THOSE
THINGS!
I'd be a Which-What-Who!

If I could be a Which-What-Who,
I'd jump high in the air.
I'd splash and spout
and run about.
I'd give the town a scare!

BUT . . .

The people would not like it.

They would be so scared, I bet,

they would call the town policemen.

They would catch me in a net!

They would put me in the zoo house
with my horns and nose and feet.
And hay, just hay,
two times a day
is all I'd get to eat.

LION

I think I would be very sad
when people came to call.
SO . . .
I don't think
a Which-What-Who
would be much fun at all.

AND SO . . .

I think

there are some things

I do not wish to be.

And that is why

I think that I

just wish to be like ME.

WACKY WEDNESDAY

By Dr. Seuss*

*writing as
Theo. LeSieg

Illustrated by George Booth

It all began

with that shoe on the wall.

A shoe on a wall . . . ?

Shouldn't be there at all!

Then I
looked up.
And I said,
"Oh, MAN!"

And that's how
Wacky Wednesday
began.

I looked out
the window.
And I said,
"GEE!"

More things were wacky!
And I saw three.

I went
down the hall
and I said,
"HEY!"

Three
more things
were wacky today!

In the
bathroom,
MORE!

In the
bathroom,
FOUR!

I began to dress.
Then I said,
"WOW!"

Four MORE things
were wacky now!

I looked
in the kitchen.
I said,
"By cracky!
Five more things
are very wacky!"

I was late for school.

I started along.

And I saw that

six more things were wrong.

BREAD

YZI-SN

And then seven more!

And the Sutherland sisters!
They looked wacky, too.

They said,

"Nothing is wacky

around here but you!"

"But look!" I yelled.
"Eight things are wrong
here at school."

"Nothing is wrong,"

they said.

"Don't be a fool."

I ran into school.

I yelled to Miss Bass . . .

. . . "Look!
Nine things
are wacky
right here
in your class!"

"Nothing is wacky
here in my class!
Get out!
You're the wacky one!
OUT!"
said Miss Bass.

I went out

the school door.

Things were worse than before.

I couldn't believe it.

Ten wacky things more!

GEORGE
WASHINGTON

Then I
counted
ELEVEN!

FOUR SALE

Then . . .
twelve WORSE things!
I got scared.
And I ran.

I ran
and knocked over
Patrolman McGann.

"I'm sorry, Patrolman."

That's all I could say.

"Don't be sorry," he smiled.

"It's that kind of a day.

But be glad!

Wacky Wednesday

will soon go away!"

"Only twenty things more
will be wacky," he said.

"Just find them
and then
you can go
back to bed."

Wacky Wednesday was gone
when I counted them all.
And I even got rid
of that shoe on the wall.

Want to be a ticket taker?

Want to be a pizza maker?

Lobsterman

Jockey

TV fixer

Ballet dancer

Soda mixer

Do you want to be an astronaut?

Or keeper of the zoo?

You've got to do something.
What DO you want to do?

Tailor?

Sailor?

Nailer?

Jailer?

You've got to BE someone
sooner or later.

How about
a wrestler . . .

a writer . . .

or a waiter?

How about
a dentist?

How about
a florist?

How about
a forester working in a forest?

Do you wish to be an oil refiner?

Diamond miner?   Dress designer?

How about a paper hanger?

How about a bass drum banger?

Do you want to do your work outdoors?

Do you want to work inside?

Would you like to be a plumber . . .

a policeman . . .

or
a bride?

Would you rather work
in a mountain town . . .

or in the desert
lower down?

Pet shop owner

Money loaner

How about
a
slide tromboner?

How about a perfume smeller?

How about a fortune teller?

You could be a turkey farmer.

You could be a teacher.

You could be a lot of things.

How about a preacher?

You could be a clown!

Or a coffee perker!

How about
an iron worker?

Fireman

Tireman

Telephone wireman

Some girls make good picture framers.

Some girls make
good lion tamers.

Some guys make
good
tightrope walkers.

Other guys
are better talkers.

Maybe you should fly a jet.

Maybe you should be a vet.

How about a deep-sea diver?

How about a beehive hiver?

Would you like to be an actor?

Would you like to run a tractor?

Like to drive a taxicab? ...

Or run a big computer lab?

Tennis pro . . .

Optometrist

Hockey pro . . .

Podiatrist

Chemist . . .

Lepidopterist

Glass blower

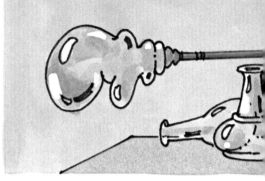

Mushroom grower

How about

a

fishbone boner

or a

roller coaster

owner?

Would you sooner

be a ballooner

or a grand-piano tuner?

Olympic champion?

Mountain guide?

It's not easy to decide.

You've got to be someone!
You can't just be a doodler.

You could be
a sculptor . . .

or, perhaps,
a noodle noodler.

You might be
a mystery guy!

Would you like
to be a spy?

Maybe you should be a vester . . .

a jester

or

a

hammock

tester.

Maybe you should be a voice.

Someday you must make a choice.
Maybe you should be a FOICE!

? ? ? ? ?

When you find out
what a FOICE is,
you can tell us
what your choice is.

I Am NOT Going to Get up Today!

By Dr. Seuss
illustrated by James Stevenson

Please let me be.

Please go away.

I am NOT going to get up today!

The alarm can ring.

The birds can peep.

My bed is warm.

My pillow's deep.

Today's the day I'm going to sleep.

I don't care if kids are getting up
right now all over town.
I'm the kid who ISN'T getting up.
I'm staying down.

All around the world
they're getting up.
And that's okay with me.
Let the kids get up in Switzerland
...or Memphis, Tennessee.

Let the kids get up in Alaska

...and in China.
I don't care.

Let the kids get up in Italy.

Let the kids get up in Spain.

Let them get up in Massachusetts

and Connecticut and Maine.

Let the kids get up in London

and in Paris and Berlin.

Let them get up all they want to.

But not me.

I'm sleeping in.

I've never been so sleepy
since I can't remember when.

You can take away my breakfast.

Give my egg back to the hen.

Nobody's going to get me up,
no matter what he does.

Today's my day for
WOOZY–SNOOZY
ZIZZ–ZIZZ
ZIZZ
ZAZZ
ZUZZ.

You can tickle my feet.
You can shake my bed.

You can pour cold water on my head.

But you're wasting your time.

So go away!

I am NOT going to get up today!

In bed is where I'm going to stay.

And I don't care what the neighbors say!

I never liked them anyway.

Let them try to wake me.

Let them scream and yowl and yelp.

They can yelp from now till Christmas

but it isn't going to help.

My bed is warm.

My pillow's deep.

Today's the day I'm going to sleep.

I don't choose to be up walking.

I don't choose to be up talking.

The only thing I'm choosing

is to lie here woozy-snoozing.

So won't you kindly go away.

I am NOT going to get up today!

You won't get me up
with a Strawberry Flip.
You won't get me up
with a Marshmallow Dip
or a Pineapple Butterscotch Ding Dang Doo!
My tongue is asleep.
And my teeth are too.

You can try with dogs and roosters.
You can try with goats and geese.
But I'm going to go on snoozing.
You can bring in the police.

You can print it in the papers.

Spread the news all over town.

But nothing's going to get me up.

Today I'm staying down.

You can shoot at me with peas and beans!
You can bring in the United States Marines!

You can put the whole thing on TV.
But I won't get up today!
Not me!

Nothing's going to get me up.
Why can't you understand!
You'll only waste your money
if you hire a big brass band.

That's why I say,

"Please go away!

I am NOT going to get up today!"

I guess he really means it.

So you can have the egg.

BEGINNER BOOKS
by Dr. Seuss
writing as Theo. LeSieg

COME OVER TO MY HOUSE

I WISH THAT I HAD DUCK FEET

MAYBE YOU SHOULD FLY A JET!
MAYBE YOU SHOULD BE A VET!

PLEASE TRY TO REMEMBER THE FIRST OF OCTEMBER!

TEN APPLES UP ON TOP!

WACKY WEDNESDAY

BRIGHT AND EARLY BOOKS
by Dr. Seuss
writing as Theo. LeSieg

THE EYE BOOK

GREAT DAY FOR UP

HOOPER HUMPERDINK . . . ? NOT HIM!

I CAN WRITE! A BOOK BY ME, MYSELF

IN A PEOPLE HOUSE

THE TOOTH BOOK

WOULD YOU RATHER BE A BULLFROG?